◆ ◆ ◆ ◆ ◆ ◆

Victor's
Quest

◆ ◆ ◆ ◆ ◆ ◆

Victor's Quest

PAMELA FREEMAN

illustrated by

KIM GAMBLE

WALKER
BOOKS

First published in Great Britain 2009 by Walker Books Ltd
87 Vauxhall Walk, London SE11 5HJ

2 4 6 8 10 9 7 5 3 1

Text © 1996 Pamela Freeman
Illustrations © 1996 Kim Gamble

The right of Pamela Freeman and Kim Gamble to be identified as
author and illustrator respectively of this work has been asserted by them
in accordance with the Copyright, Designs and Patents Act 1988

This book has been typeset in StempelSchneidler

Printed in Great Britain by Clays Ltd, St Ives plc

British Library Cataloguing in Publication Data:
a catalogue record for this book is available from the British Library

ISBN 978-1-4063-0248-6

www.walker.co.uk

For my niece, Megan
P.F.

1 ◆ ◆ ◆ "My mother's sending me on a quest," Prince Victor said gloomily. He bit into the pumpkin scone

◆ ◆ ◆ Marigold had just handed him. "Mum says if I'm going to take over the queendom from her I have to find myself a princess to marry who'll show a bit of sense."

He finished the scone and reached for another. "I don't see why," he said. "All I'll ever have to do as King of Serendipity is open parliament and make speeches at fêtes. Still" – he sighed – "that was what she said I've got to do."

"How is your mother?" Marigold asked.

"Sick," Victor said. "She says the idea of handing the queendom over to me has given her palpitations. So she's sending me on a quest." He looked hopefully up at Marigold. "And I've come to you for help."

"I'm just the palace gardener," Marigold said. "Quests are more in a wizard's line. Why don't you ask the court wizard for help?"

"He thinks I'm stupid," Victor said.

8

"Victor," Marigold said kindly, "you *are* stupid."

"I know, but when you say it I don't mind. The court wizard makes me feel *really* stupid."

"Where are you going?" Marigold asked.

"Into the Great Bog of Cloone. Or the Dark Forest of Nevermore. Or the Wuthering Uplands of Woebegone. Somewhere like that. You know."

9

"Well … I'm not sure that anything I've got will help. My kind of magic takes months to work. And even then it's just natural magic. But I'll give you what I have," Marigold said. She disappeared into her stillroom where she made medicines from the herbs and plants of the palace gardens. She came out with a selection of small, coloured bottles and jars.

"Now look and listen; hear and remember, Victor. This is what I'll send with you." She put a small blue bottle on the table. "This is woundwort – a very good antiseptic. If you get cut or hurt, wash the wound and put this

on, then tie a clean cloth over it. All right?
See, I've put the name on the label."

Victor nodded. "Woundwort. I'll remember
that."

"And this is feverfew." She opened a squat
white jar which had something that looked
like tea leaves inside. "If you get a fever, make
a tisane out of this – that's like a tea. Tie some
of it up in a bit of cloth and let it soak in
boiling water for a while, then drink
it sweetened with honey. OK?"

"With honey. OK," Victor said.

"This is eye balm." Marigold set down a small pot of pink ointment and showed Victor how to put on the cap. "Turn it tightly. If it gets dust in it, it's useless. This is for when your eyes are tired from looking into the sun all day. Rub it lightly on your eyelids. On the *outside*, Victor."

Victor nodded.

"And this one," Marigold said, handing him a green bottle, "is rose water and glycerine. I don't know why I'm giving you this, but maybe you'd better have a present for the princess when you meet her. It's a hand lotion. To make hands soft."

"Hands." Victor nodded again. "Present for the princess. Good. Thank you, Marigold." He sighed. "I suppose I'd better get started."

"Now listen, Victor; listen well. On a quest, the smartest brains won't always help you. Remember the old rules: be kind, be polite to everyone you meet, and be pure of heart.

12

And you're all those things," Marigold said firmly, reaching up to kiss his cheek.

Victor blushed.

2 ◆ ◆ ◆ ◆ Victor was a tall young man, broad
in the shoulder, with large steady
hands, brown eyes and brown hair.
◆ ◆ ◆ ◆ On this particular day he carried
apples and cheese and good brown bread in
his backpack, as well as a few extra pumpkin
scones with butter. And like all princes off on
a quest, he wore a sword and rode a horse.
Not the big white charger his mother had
wanted him to take, but his old chestnut
mare, Quince.

"Maybe it's just as well," the Queen had sighed. "That horse has more sense than Victor ever will." And for once she was right.

Victor decided to go through the Dark Forest of Nevermore. He was very brave.

The Dark Forest of Nevermore was a pine forest, with huge towering trees reaching up for the sun. They were so tall that only the topmost branches ever got any light and all the lower

branches died off and turned rusty orange.

Victor rode along a forest path between bare dark trunks patched with grey and orange lichen, while high above him the spiny green branches sighed mournfully. A person with imagination riding through this forest would think about ghosts and wailing banshees, and would get very nervous waiting for *something* to drop down out of the branches.

Victor had almost no imagination. What he was mostly thinking about was how long it would be before he could honestly say, "Well, I guess it's lunchtime," and stop for a bite.

In between thinking about the pumpkin scones and the apples, he was thinking about the princess he was supposed to be finding, and hoping that she wouldn't be the kind of person who made him feel *really* stupid.

On the whole he wasn't paying a great deal of attention – which is often a mistake in the Dark Forest of Nevermore.

So he was quite surprised when *something* swooped down out of the trees above him.

3 ♦ ♦ ♦ ♦   The *something* launched itself at Victor's head. Quince darted forward and Victor ducked, so the *something* missed and smacked straight into the trunk of the tree next to him.

It bounced off and fell to the ground and sat there, wailing.

"Oh, cumquats and castor oil!" it said. "I'll never get it right."

19

It wasn't very big, now that Victor had time to look at it more closely, but it had fairly large talons on its feet and wicked-looking clawed hands. It was furry – an orangey fur like the lichens on the trees – and it had a small pointed head like a bat's and large ears like a bat's and leathery sort of wings like a bat's…

"Are you a bat?" Victor asked.

"What do I look like?" the creature asked right back.

"You look like a bat," Victor said. "A big orange bat."

"Top marks. Go to the head of the class.

20

I am a bat. A Very Large and Ferocious Orange Bat of the Dark Forest of Nevermore." The bat struggled to his feet and looked despairingly up at Victor. "And now I suppose you're going to kill me," he said.

"Is that something I should do?" Victor asked warily.

"That's what most people do when a bat tries to take their head off and misses."

"Does that happen often?" Victor asked.

"More often than you'd think," the bat answered glumly, and started poking around in the fur on his shoulder. He winced.

"You're hurt!" Victor said.

21

"Of course I'm hurt," the bat answered testily. "I slammed into that tree trunk at attack speed. I got a twig in the shoulder."

Victor jumped off his horse and rummaged in his backpack. He pulled out the small pink pot. "I've got some stuff here for wounds."

Quince butted him with her nose and shook her head.

"I haven't got some stuff here for wounds?" Victor said tentatively. Quince shook her head and nosed in the backpack. Victor looked again and took out the small blue bottle.

He read the label carefully. "Woundwort.

This is the stuff for wounds. But Marigold said you've got to clean the wound first. Have you got any water?"

The bat stared at him. "You're going to help me?"

"Of course," Victor said. "Where's the water?"

"Um … this way." The bat turned and waddled off through the forest. He kept shaking his head and looking over his shoulder as Victor got on Quince and followed him.

When they came to a small stream the bat sat down on a rock and grimaced while Victor cleaned the wound, smeared on a good dose of woundwort, and then tied his handkerchief over the top.

"It's quite clean," he told the bat. "I haven't used it yet."

The bat stared at him, and then seemed to make up his mind. "I'm Carruthers," he said.

"How do you do?" Victor said. "I am Victor, Prince of Serendipity."

"I'm not at all surprised," Carruthers said. "Look, you'll have to go carefully through the rest of the forest. There are a lot of Ferocious Orange Bats around, and they have much better aim than me." He thought about it for a while. Victor waited patiently. "I think I'll have to come with you. Escort you through the rest of the bat territory. That seems fair."

"All right," Victor said. "Do you think it's time for lunch yet?"

So they had lunch. Carruthers had never eaten pumpkin scones before and was quite taken with them – so much so that Victor only had half a scone and Carruthers ate five and a half. Victor ate an apple instead. Then he climbed on Quince and hoisted Carruthers up to perch on his saddle-bow, and they went back to the path while Victor told Carruthers all about his quest.

Every so often, as they cantered along the dark and gloomy forest paths, Carruthers took out a silver whistle and blew into it. Victor couldn't hear any noise come out of it, though.

"Bats can hear much higher sounds than humans," Carruthers explained. "So can dogs and lots of other animals. I'm just warning off the other bats. There's a system of signals: one blow for 'stay away', two blows for 'come here', and three for 'there's a fight on and everyone should come and help'."

Eventually they came to the end of the pine forest. Before them was a different kind of forest – beech trees turning golden and brown for autumn. Victor thought this was rather strange, as it had been high summer when he had left Marigold's, and he'd only been gone a day.

"Oh, that's the forest for you," Carruthers said. "Time is very odd in here. It's been high noon in the beech forest for months now." He took the silver whistle from round his neck. "Here. You take it. You can do with all the help you can get."

Victor was touched. He thought for a moment and then said, "There's not much I can do to thank you, but I am a prince and I can make you a knight. Would you like to be Sir Carruthers?"

"A Sir?" Carruthers brushed some imaginary dirt from his fur. "Well, if you insist…"

So Victor knighted Carruthers on the forest floor, and then rode off into the bright sunshine and golden leaves of the beech forest.

"Be careful!" Sir Carruthers shouted after him. "And watch out for the eagles!"

4 ◆ ◆ ◆ ◆ Quince plodded on along a faint path. Victor felt cheerful. This forest of bright sunshine and golden leaves ◆ ◆ ◆ ◆ was much nicer than the Dark Forest of Nevermore. It was, if anything, a little *too* bright. Victor found himself squinting against the glare. Quince walked along with her eyes almost shut. Gradually it grew so bright that they could scarcely see at all.

Which was why Victor heard the voices before he saw the eagles.

"Now, I'm sure, my sisters, that we're all agreed. None of us, least of all *me*, wants to move to that gloomy, perpetually dreary pine forest. But something *must be done*. Why, only yesterday I attempted a brief sortie against the ravens and within five minutes I was blinded. *I*, the eagle chief!"

Quince stopped. Peering through the trees, Victor saw a dead oak tree in the middle of a clearing. And on the tree he could just make out a number of large birds. Eagles. Quite a few, in fact: about thirty. And the one perched

on the topmost branch was still talking. "My sisters, something *must be done*."

"What?" a voice asked. "Time has been stuck at high noon for months now. We don't know when it will start moving again. If you ask me, that witch has something to do with it."

"She says she is not a witch," the first eagle replied. "In any case, nothing we can say will affect her. What we need is something to help us withstand the sun. How can we be eagles if we *can't see*?"

"Um … excuse me," Victor said. Quince snorted and shook her head, but she moved forward into the clearing anyway.

Victor remembered this time that the eye balm was in the small pink pot.

"There's not very much of it," he said apologetically. "But it might help."

The eagles, who were affronted at first that a mere human would interrupt their council, unbent sufficiently to let Victor put the ointment on their eyelids.

"On the outside," Victor said, pleased at having remembered.

The relief was immediate.

"Oh, bliss!" the eagle chief said. "My name is Nancy, first among the eagles."

"How do you do?" Victor said. "I am Victor, Prince of Serendipity."

"Victor," Nancy said, "this has been very kind of you, my dear boy, and don't think for a moment we aren't grateful. But it's just a stopgap measure, you understand. Until we can get Time to move on, we still have the same problem. Unless we act now while we can all see."

32

"Um … yes," said Victor.

"So that's settled then. I will lead you to the witch and you will … deal with her."

"A witch?" Victor said uneasily.

"My dear boy," Nancy exclaimed, "you're not *afraid*?"

Victor scratched behind his ear. "No," he said. "Not recently. But I don't know much about witches. They're supposed to be smart, aren't they?"

"What difference does that make?" Nancy asked scornfully.

Victor shrugged. "Oh, all right. Show me the way."

Nancy flew ahead of Quince for about twenty minutes until they came to the edge of the beech forest. It was still high noon, but on the other side of the clearing from where they stood, they could see twilight creeping up among gum trees. In the middle of the clearing, by a small stream, stood a cottage. Quite a pretty cottage, Victor thought. It was made

of wood and had large friendly windows,
and flowers and herbs planted all around.

"That's nice," he said.

"It doesn't always look like that," Nancy
said darkly. "Now go ahead and deal with the
witch, my dear boy, and you shall have the
eagles' undying gratitude."

So Victor rode forward into the clearing.

Immediately an old woman came out of the cottage. And she was the very type and pattern of a witch. She was bent and old and ragged; she wore dark clothes and had scraggy, unkempt hair and gnarled old hands, and she peered up at him from under craggy eyebrows.

"Well, Prince Victor," she said. "What can I do for you?"

5 ◆ ◆ ◆ ◆ Victor was not surprised that she knew his name. He had grown up with everyone knowing who he ◆ ◆ ◆ ◆ was. So he swung down off Quince, and said, "How do you do? The eagles have sent me to ask you to stop it being high noon and let Time run again."

The witch laughed. "Oh, they have, have they? I suppose they told you I was a witch?"

"That's right," Victor said.

"Well, I'm not," the old woman snapped. "I'm an enchanter. That's entirely different."

"Oh," Victor said. "I see."

The old woman glared at him and he tried to think of something else to say.

"I like your rosemary bush," he said at last. "And your sage. And your calendula."

"How do you know so much about plants,

and you a prince?" the enchanter asked
suspiciously.

"Friend of mine taught me," Victor said.
He noticed that the enchanter was rubbing
her hands together, over and over again. This
looked rather disagreeable, as though she was
expecting some nasty treat to come along.

She saw him looking. "I suppose you've
noticed my hands," she said. "Go ahead, say
what you think. I know they're ugly."

"Ugly?" Victor asked.

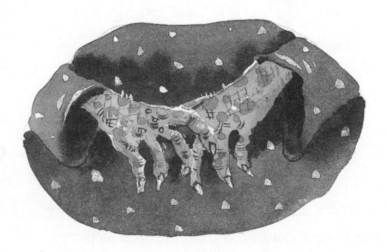

"Rough and horrible. Oh, yes. It's a spell, you know. I tried a bit of necromancy and it backfired on me. Serves me right," she said gloomily. "Should have known better."

She held out her hands to Victor. "See how rough and sore they are? Nothing can help. I've tried everything."

Victor coughed. "Um … have you tried rose water and glycerine?"

"Noooo," the enchanter said slowly. "I don't believe I have." A crafty look came into her eyes. "I don't suppose you have some? Why don't you come inside and rest, poor tired prince?"

Quince butted him in the back, but even Victor wasn't that stupid.

"No, thank you," he said. "But I do have some. I'd be glad to give it to you, if…"

"I know," the old woman said. "If I start Time up again. Well, I'll make a deal with you. You give me the lotion, and I'll start Time up. But you've got to tell those dratted eagles to stay away from my rabbits and chickens."

She pointed to where, behind the cottage, there were chicken runs and rabbit warrens. "They seemed to think I was running a restaurant for them!" she said bitterly. "I had to send all my chickens away. Making it high noon all the time was the only way I could protect my other animals. But, to tell you the truth, I was getting a bit tired of it myself."

So Victor gave her the rose-water lotion and she applied it eagerly to her cracked hands. And as they grew smoother, so did she. Instead of being an old, ugly, unkempt woman, she became an old, handsome and tidy one. She straightened up; her hair grew bouncier and smoother; her nose grew shorter – and her hands grew positively soft. She smiled at Victor.

"Let me give you two pieces of advice," she said. "Never dabble in necromancy and beware of the Dolorous Mist of Tranby."

"What's that?" Victor asked.

"You'll know it when you see it," the enchanter said, and disappeared into thin air.

Only her voice was left behind. "Don't forget to tell the eagles!" it said, and then it too faded away.

Victor went back to the woods as the evening shadows began to drop rapidly over the beech forest. Everywhere birds were chattering and singing, animals were appearing from the undergrowth, and the eagles were shrieking happily.

He gave Nancy the enchanter's message.

"Oh, very well," Nancy grumbled. "But what

people expect when they put a chicken run in the middle of eagle territory I don't know... Well, thank you, Queen's son. If you ever need the help of the eagles, just call out with all your might. We will hear. Or wave. We might see you. Goodbye, dear."

And she flew away.

Quince and Victor were both tired. So they made camp next to a small stream and went comfortably to sleep, ignoring the strange rustlings in the bushes and the odd hoots and howls from the trees above. It was the first night for months, and the night creatures were having the time of their lives.

◆ ◆ ◆ ◆ It might have been an owl, and

6 then again it might not, that woke
Victor sometime before dawn.
◆ ◆ ◆ ◆ It shrieked and flapped very loudly
next to his ear, then flew away before he was
properly awake. Quince neighed in fear, and
turned to run away, but Victor caught her.

"Settle down, girl," he said. "Whatever it was,
it's gone now. Nothing to be afraid of." And
because it was growing grey with morning,
he saddled her up, fished the last apple out
of his pack and rode away munching.

That day he rode through a eucalypt forest,
through the blue-gum scent and the sharp
tang of boronia, with the ferns brushing
Quince's knees, and the tops of the gum
trees creamy with blossom. It was a scrubby,
untidy forest, very different from the darkling
pines or the golden beech, but Victor liked it.
It suited his mood, which was happy-go-lucky
and we'll-see-what-happens-next. He rode

along whistling and thinking wistfully of the
five and a half pumpkin scones Carruthers
had eaten the day before.

Later he came out into a rolling plain ringed
with mountains. In the centre of the plain was
a steep, rocky hill – almost a mountain, craggy,
and difficult to climb. Around the base of the
hill was a band of water. In the setting sun the
water glinted silver. Victor put his hand up to

shade his eyes and wished he hadn't used all the eye balm on the eagles. He and Quince went on towards the hill, because the last thing his mother had said to him was, "On a quest you must always look for the unusual" – and this hill was definitely unusual.

As the sun slid down behind the mountains, Victor saw a small wisp of fog start to rise from the water. As it rose it seemed to draw more fog with it, until it was a definite ball of mist that drifted over the water backwards and forwards, as if it were seeking something. And as it drifted it seemed to sing.

It wasn't a pleasant song. It had no words, but even so Victor knew it was a song about all the sad things of life. As he listened to its wailing and whining, he thought about every sorrowful time he could remember; and he was surprised at how many sad times there had been. He found himself crying helplessly. He cried so hard that he almost slid off Quince's back. But he clung on to her warm neck for comfort, and that was what saved him. Because Quince, realizing that Victor was fast turning into a slobbering wreck, spun round and set off back towards the gum trees. And as they left, Victor heard a girl's voice float down from the top of the mountain.

"Oh, no, don't go! Please don't go!" it said. Victor thought he had never heard anything so soft or longing. He tried to turn Quince around so he could see the person who belonged to the voice, but Quince wouldn't be turned. And by the time he had reached

the gum trees, Victor thought that Quince
might have been right.

They camped that night under the gums and
Victor tried not to think about food. Quince
munched happily on grass and shrubbery, but
Victor had nothing left. To take his mind off
food, he talked to Quince about the girl's voice.

"I know you think it was part of the
Dolorous Mist of Tranby – I suppose that
was the Dolorous Mist?"

Quince nodded and went on munching.
"But what if it wasn't? Part of the mist,
I mean. What if it really was a girl – a princess
– in trouble, waiting for me to rescue her?
That's what I'm here for. No, Quince, I don't
care what you say, we're going to have to go
back there tomorrow morning."

But in the morning Quince wouldn't let
Victor even mount her, let alone get within
earshot of the mist. She kept butting her head
at his pocket and whinnying. Finally he gave
in and sat down.

"All right," he said. "There's something in my pocket you want. Let's have a look." And he pulled out a little parcel of apple seeds he meant to take back to Marigold, a second clean handkerchief, a penknife, seven assorted coins, two dragon's teeth, and Carruthers's silver whistle.

Quince snorted three times.

"Three times?" Victor said. "But that means there's a fight on and everyone should come and help."

Quince nodded.

"You're sure?" Victor asked her. She nodded emphatically.

"OK. If you say so." And he blew the whistle three times, hard.

They waited for a few minutes, and for a few minutes more. Then Victor said, "I suppose it *is* a long way from the pine forest. We'll just give them half an hour – and then we'll go anyway, right?" And in half an hour he said, "They could have got lost; I'd better blow it again," and he did. Half an hour after that he was asleep with his head on his arms, and he didn't wake up until lunchtime, which was when Carruthers arrived.

Not just Carruthers. It was Carruthers plus two hundred and seventy-one Very Large and Ferocious Orange Bats, all looking for a fight. Victor woke up to find them gathered around and glaring at him.

"Well?" said Carruthers. "Where's the fight?"

"It was Quince's idea," Victor said. He explained about the Dolorous Mist of Tranby.

Carruthers waddled over to Quince. "You want us to fly him to the top of the mountain? Over the top so the mist can't get at him?"

Quince nodded.

"That's a great idea, Quince," Victor said.

Carruthers started talking to the other bats in a very high, squeaky voice which Victor could barely hear. They didn't look too happy at first, but eventually they started shrugging and saying things like, "It'll be a first, I suppose" and "This is a one-off, understand?" and "Just because he made you a Sir doesn't mean you can boss us around; we're just doing you a favour, see?" and Victor knew they'd agreed.

It took twenty bats to fly Victor towards the mountain, with Quince following along on the ground. As they flew over the mist, Victor heard its sad song float up to meet him and he started sobbing for the teddy bear he had lost in the stables when he was three. But the bats just gripped him more firmly and flew higher, and after a while he remembered that his mother had found the teddy bear the next day and that everything had been all right.

By that time they were at the top of the mountain. The bats lowered him to the ground, panting.

"You ain't half heavy, mate," one of them said. "Good luck." And they all flew away before he could thank them. So he got his spare handkerchief out and wiped his eyes and looked around him.

♦ ♦ ♦ ♦ On the top of the mountain there

7 was a garden. Not up to Marigold's
standards, perhaps, but very nice

♦ ♦ ♦ ♦ all the same. It ran to flowers: roses
and daffodils and jonquils and snowdrops
and azaleas and lady's slippers and pansies
and violets and daphne, all blooming at the
same time, so Victor knew it was magic. In
the centre of the garden was a house. A fairly
ordinary brick house, with two windows
beside a front door, and a little verandah on
the side with a rocking chair on it. The only

odd thing, Victor realized as he looked about, was the tall wooden fence that surrounded the garden – so tall he couldn't see over it.

From behind the fence came the strangest noises he had ever heard. It sounded as if a very large *something* was outside. *Something* that scratched and hissed with a thousand voices, *something* that screeched and cried with a thousand more, *something* that rubbed up against the fence like a slithering, feathery, scaly, enormous snake.

For the first time in his life, Victor was not feeling brave. There was something about that noise that took all his courage away. He gulped, and looked back at the house.

On the verandah now there was a girl. His princess. Had to be. She stood with her hand on the verandah post. She was pretty and she looked intelligent and resourceful and very, very puzzled.

"Who are you?" she asked. It was the same voice that Victor had heard the day before,

floating down from the mist. He beamed,
his fear forgotten.

"I'm Victor, Prince of Serendipity," he said,
and he stared at her as she came closer. She
had light brown hair cut very short and blue
eyes that looked as though they could have
withstood the sun in the beech forest without
any eye balm. She had a mouth that looked
as if it smiled a lot, and her voice was closer
to the wind in the trees than Victor had ever
realized a voice could be.

"How did you get up here?" the princess said.

"Some orange bats brought me."

"Right."

"Are you a prisoner here, fair maiden?"
Victor sighed happily. He'd been waiting for
years to say that line. His mother had taught
it to him.

"Well," the princess said, "not exactly.
It's just that it's rather difficult to get out with
all *that* going on." And she waved her hand
towards the fence.

Once again Victor became aware of the
hissing, scratching noise. It seemed to get louder
as he listened. It sounded like a particularly
nasty, vicious, hungry, horrible *thing*. He drew
in a deep breath. This was the time for all those
lessons in being princely to pay off. This was
the time when he confronted the monster and
killed it for the sake of the fair damsel. He'd just
have to pretend he was brave.

So Victor drew his sword and marched
towards the gate.

"Where are you going?" the princess said.

"To kill the monster who is keeping you prisoner," he told her. He gulped. "Right away."

"Hold on," the princess said. She caught up with him and looked him up and down. "You're going to kill the monster?"

Victor nodded.

"With the sword?"

He nodded again.

"You're afraid of it."

Victor hung his head and blushed.

"But you're going to try to kill it anyway."

He nodded yet again.

The princess bit her lip. "What if you get killed?"

Victor shrugged.

"Hmm," the princess said. "Why don't you come inside and have lunch first?"

Lunch was very good. There was fresh baked bread and home-cured ham, there was scrambled eggs with chives, and potatoes baked with bacon and cream. There was hot apple crumble and custard, and fresh figs and cheese for afters. Victor ate a lot. And all the time he ate, the princess stared at him.

"What happens after you kill the monster?" she asked.

"I take you home and marry you," Victor said.

"Don't you think you'd better ask me first? I might not want to get married."

"But that's how it always happens. I'm on a quest to find a princess to marry. Now I've found one, I kill the monster and marry you."

"Victor," the princess said, "I hate to tell you this, but I'm not a princess."

Victor stopped eating. "No?" he said.

"No," she said.

Victor thought about this for some time, and then smiled. "You will be after you marry me," he announced happily. Then he looked anxiously at her. "That is … if you want to."

She smiled kindly at him. "You know, I just might want to do that. My name's Valerian." She leaned forward and kissed him. He spilt his custard.

64

"That's not supposed to happen until *after* I kill the monster."

"Ye-es, I know … but I'm afraid there isn't any monster."

"But … what about…"

Valerian shrugged apologetically. "It's just the chickens."

"The *chickens*?"

She nodded. "Of course, they are rather *large* chickens. And very … aggressive. They keep me penned up here almost as well as if they were a real monster. But they're not.

They're just a plague that an enchanter set on me because I had nicer hands than she did."

And indeed, Victor had noticed that she had very nice hands. "I use rose water on them," she explained.

Victor nodded sagely. "And glycerine," he said.

"That's right!" she exclaimed. "How did you know? Anyway, I can't come with you unless we can get rid of the chickens – and I don't think your sword will do you much good. There're too many of them."

They went to peek through the fence, and Victor saw that Valerian was right. There was a mass of chickens – not just hundreds, but thousands of chickens, all clucking and hissing and scratching in the dirt.

They were very large and nasty chickens. They had glaring red eyes and big pointy beaks and bedraggled yellow feathers. And they were vicious. As soon as they saw Valerian and Victor looking through the fence, they started hissing and clucking and trying to gouge their eyes out through the palings. They climbed up on top of each other to get at them.

And they smelled disgusting. They smelled worse than anything Victor had ever smelled. He might be able to kill a hundred or more, but he would be overwhelmed by the stench before he got even halfway through.

"They're not like *real* chickens at all, are they?" he asked.

"Oh, no," Valerian said. "They don't talk or anything. They're just part of a spell."

Victor knew that somewhere in the back of his mind he knew the solution. So he sat down in the rocking chair and thought about it.

"What we need..." he said in mid-afternoon...

"What we need is..." he said at twilight...

"What we need," he said at dawn,
"is a flock of eagles."

"That," Valerian said as she watched him
make porridge, "is a very good idea. But flocks
of eagles aren't easy to come by. Where are
you going to find one?"

Victor took a deep breath. "Leave it to me,"
he said.

8 ◆ ◆ ◆ ◆ Victor went outside and climbed
to the top of the crag behind
Valerian's house. He cupped his
◆ ◆ ◆ ◆ hands round his mouth and yelled
with all his might and breath, "NANCY! HEY,
NANCY! EAGLES! IT'S VICTOR AND I NEED YOUR
HELP!!!" He waved his arms around for ten
minutes, just to be on the safe side.

Valerian watched him. "What do we do
now?" she asked.

"We wait," Victor said. "And you can tell
me all about yourself."

71

So they went back to the verandah and
Victor sat in the rocking chair and Valerian sat
on his lap and they talked about all sorts of
things. Victor was having a better time than
he could ever remember having, so he was
almost annoyed when a screech came from
overhead and Nancy arrived and landed on
the verandah rail.

"My dear boy, you don't seem to be in
trouble to me," Nancy said. She turned to
Valerian. "Lovely lot of chickens you have
there, girlie."

"That's just it," Victor said. "How would you like to invite your friends to a chicken party?"

After Nancy had left, Victor went over to the fence and coughed loudly. The scratching and hissing increased. "Chickens! Excuse me, chickens!" Victor shouted. "I just thought you'd like to know that the eagle has gone to get a whole lot of her friends. They're planning on having a chicken party. You're the main course."

On the other side of the fence there was a sudden silence. Then with a great squawking and clucking and even a few yelps, the chickens ran, flapping their wings and tumbling down the hill as fast as they could.

Victor and Valerian watched from the verandah as they scrambled towards the woods, their tail feathers up and their heads down for speed. they disappeared into the trees just as the first of the eagles came zooming overhead.

"Do you think they'll make it?" Valerian asked.

"Well…" said Victor. "The enchanter did make a deal with the eagles so her chickens would be safe. If they can get back to the chicken run they'll be fine. And they won't bother *you* any more!"

So finally Victor, Valerian and Quince started back for Serendipity, avoiding the Dolorous Mist of Tranby by climbing down the other side of Valerian's mountain.

9 ◆ ◆ ◆ ◆   When Victor walked through
the throne-room doors holding
Valerian by the hand, his mother
◆ ◆ ◆ ◆   almost fainted.

"He's actually done it!" she said. "The boy's
gone and found himself a princess. Well done,
oh well done, Victor!"

"Valerian's not a princess," Victor said.
"But she will be after she marries me."

"*N-not* a princess?" the Queen stuttered.
"Not a *princess*?"

"Not yet," Victor said, and he held
Valerian's hand very tightly.

"You ungrateful boy!" the Queen said. "You
know what this will do to me. It will send me
into a fever! I may never recover from it."

Victor let go of Valerian's hand and
rummaged in his backpack. He held out

the jar of feverfew. "Try making a tea out of this," he said. "With honey. I'm going to take Valerian to meet Marigold."

Valerian smiled at the Queen. "He's not *really* stupid when it counts, Your Majesty," she said, and went off to meet Marigold. Who liked her almost as much as Victor did.

PAMELA FREEMAN has written
numerous books for children, including
the highly successful Floramonde series.
She has also worked as a scriptwriter for
Australia's ABC Television. She lives
in Sydney, Australia, with her family.
You can find out more about Pamela
and her books by visiting:
www.pamelafreemanbooks.com

◆ ◆ ◆ ◆ ◆ ◆ ◆

KIM GAMBLE is one of Australia's
best-loved illustrators and has won
several high-profile awards for his work,
including the Children's Book Council of
Australia Book of the Year Award.
He lives in Sydney, Australia.